ALL by MYSeLF!

written and illustrated by **ALIKI**

SCHOLASTIC INC.

New York   Toronto   London   Auckland   Sydney
Mexico City   New Delhi   Hong Kong   Buenos Aires

This book is for:

Peter (my inspiration)

John (his accomplished big brother)

Sam (who learned how)

Brittany (who is just doing it)

Alexa (her big sister), and

Panayiota (they know how, too)

ISBN 0-439-31916-1

Copyright © 2000 by Aliki Brandenberg. All rights reserved.
Published by Scholastic Inc., 555 Broadway, New York, NY 10012, by arrangement with HarperCollins Publishers. SCHOLASTIC and associated logos are trademarks and/or registered trademarks of Scholastic Inc.

12 11 10 9 8 7 6 5 4 3 2 1   1 2 3 4 5 6/0

Printed in the U.S.A.   08

First Scholastic printing, October 2001

Run to the bathroom,
fast as an elf.

Sit,

wash,

brush,

all by myself.

Down with the bottoms,

up with the top.

Down with the shirt,

and snap it all up.

Pull up the blue jeans,

button
and
zip.

On with the socks,

and now for a flip.

Right shoe,

left shoe.

Tie,

comb,

done!

Breakfast's ready,

pour,

crunch,

yum!

Open the
school door.

I'm on my way.

Build,

paint,

write,

Sing.

Fun all day.

When school is over,

there's still more to do.

Going here,

going there.

Quiet is nice, too.

Practice my lesson.

Soon time to eat.

Help with
the dinner.

Mmm,
what a treat.

A whole day is over.

Nighttime comes.

unzip,

down.

Unsnap, up,

Water runs.

Steamy, dreamy,

splash, squeeze, rub.

Clean and dry now.

Good-bye, tub.

Up with the
bottoms,

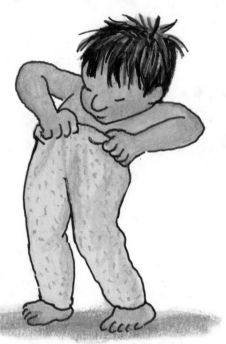

down with
the top.

Choose a book.

Snuggle close.

Time to stop.

Close the light.

Say good night.

Sleep sweet dreams.

One day ends. . .

then another begins!